Goldilocks

❖   ❖   ❖

For my mother,
Audrey,
and my son,
Rudyard,
and special thanks to Yury, Kaylie, and Clay

❖   ❖   ❖

Goldilocks

✦ **Janice Russell** ✦

Boyds Mills Press

Copyright © 1997 by Janice Russell
All rights reserved

Published by Bell Books
Boyds Mills Press, Inc.
A Highlights Company
815 Church Street
Honesdale, Pennsylvania 18431
Printed in Mexico

Publisher Cataloging-in-Publication Data
Goldilocks / Janice Russell.—1st ed.
[32]p. : col.ill. ; cm.
Summary : Traditional folk tale of a girl who enters the cottage of three bears.
ISBN 1-56397-430-4
1. Bears—Folklore—Juvenile literature. 2. Bears—Fiction—Juvenile literature. [1.
Bears—Folklore. 2. Bears—Fiction.] I. Russell, Janice, ill. II. Title.
398.2—dc20 [E] 1997 AC · CIP
Library of Congress Catalog Card Number 95-83166

First edition, 1997
Book designed by Janice Russell
The text of this book is set in 18-point Goudy.
The illustrations are done in oils.

10 9 8 7 6 5 4 3 2

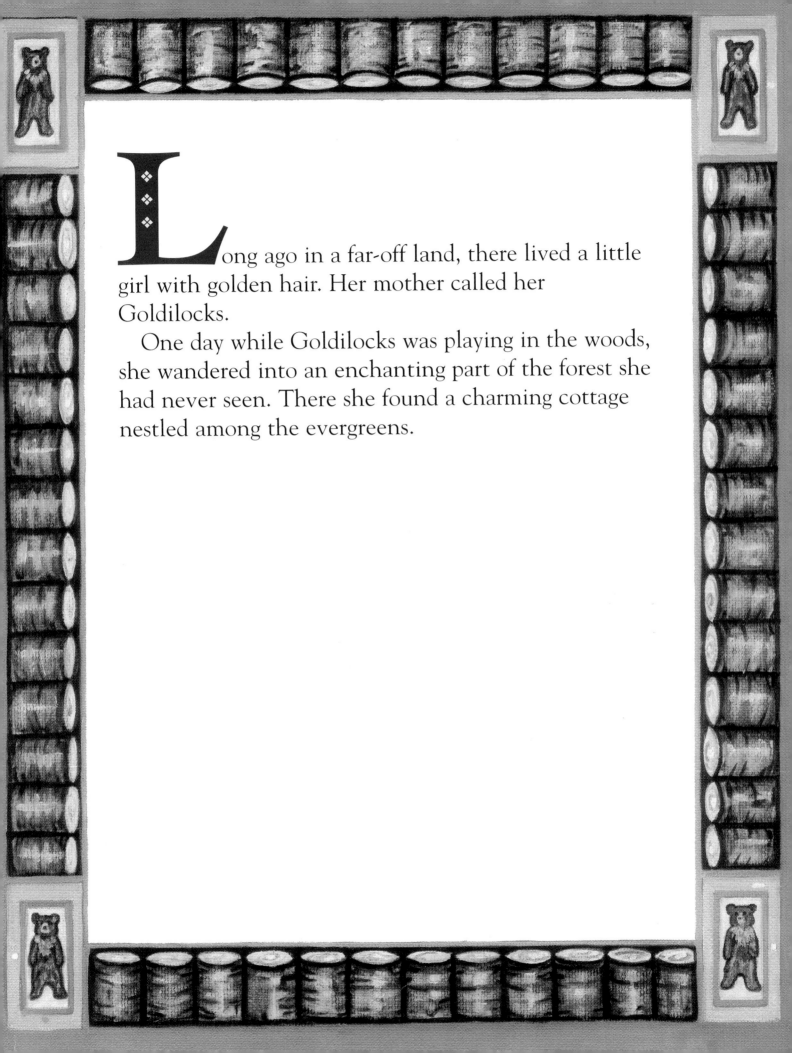

Long ago in a far-off land, there lived a little girl with golden hair. Her mother called her Goldilocks.

One day while Goldilocks was playing in the woods, she wandered into an enchanting part of the forest she had never seen. There she found a charming cottage nestled among the evergreens.

Goldilocks tiptoed around the cottage and peeked in the windows. When she saw that no one was at home, she stepped inside for a better look.

Goldilocks did not know she was in the home of three bears—Papa Bear, Mama Bear, and Baby Bear.

She saw three bowls of porridge on the kitchen table, which the bears had left to cool while they took their morning walk.

Goldilocks was hungry and the porridge smelled delicious. First she tasted the porridge in the great big bowl, which belonged to Papa Bear. But it was much too hot.

Then she tasted the porridge in the medium-size bowl, which belonged to Mama Bear. But it was much too cold. Finally she tasted the porridge in the wee small bowl, which belonged to Baby Bear. It was just right. So she ate it all up.

Goldilocks looked around the cozy parlor and saw three chairs. First she sat in the great big chair, which belonged to Papa Bear. But it was much too hard.

Then she sat in the medium-size chair, which belonged to Mama Bear. But it was much too soft.

Finally she sat in the wee small chair, which belonged to Baby Bear. It was just right. But it was so small that Goldilocks broke it.

Now Goldilocks was sleepy. She went upstairs and found a snug little bedroom with three beds. First she lay on the great big bed, which belonged to Papa Bear. But it was too high at the head.

Then she lay on the medium-size bed, which belonged to Mama Bear. But it was too low at the foot.

Finally she lay on the wee small bed, which belonged to Baby Bear. It was just right. So Goldilocks snuggled under the soft, warm blanket and fell fast asleep.

While Goldilocks was sleeping, the three bears returned from their morning walk. They were very hungry.

But as soon as Papa Bear looked in his bowl, he said in his great big voice, "Someone has been eating my porridge."

Mama Bear looked in her bowl and said in her medium-size voice, "Someone has been eating my porridge as well."

Then Baby Bear said in his wee small voice, "Someone has been eating my porridge, too, and ate it all up."

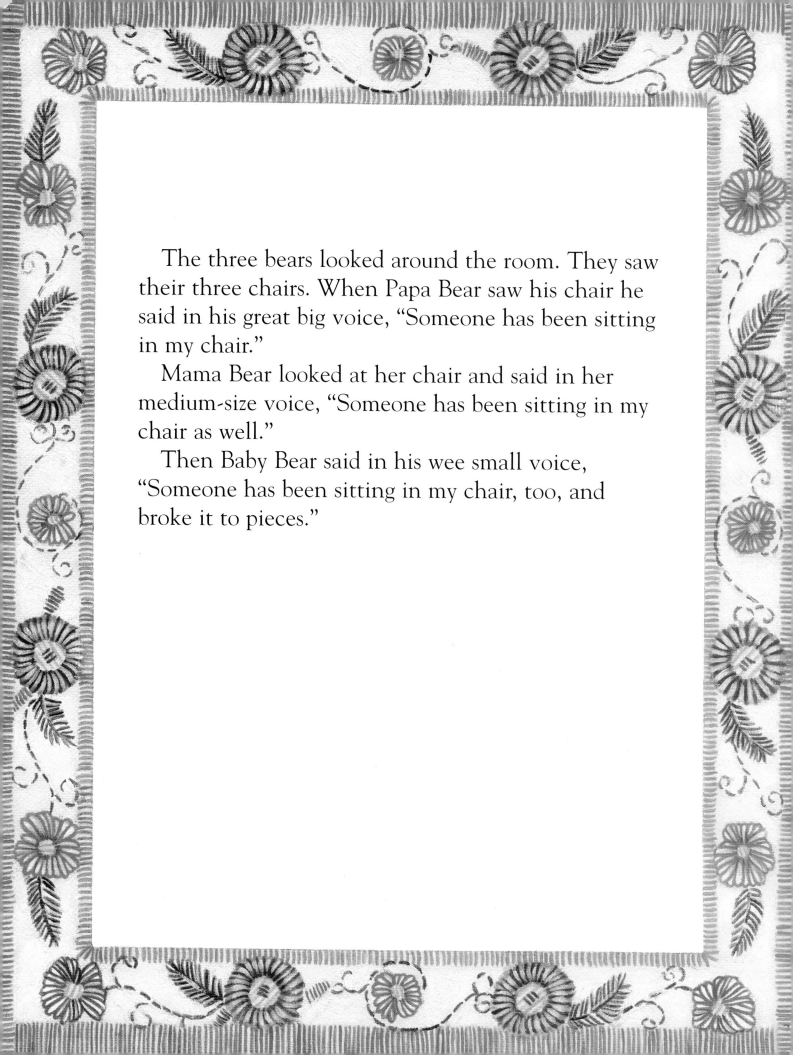

The three bears looked around the room. They saw their three chairs. When Papa Bear saw his chair he said in his great big voice, "Someone has been sitting in my chair."

Mama Bear looked at her chair and said in her medium-size voice, "Someone has been sitting in my chair as well."

Then Baby Bear said in his wee small voice, "Someone has been sitting in my chair, too, and broke it to pieces."

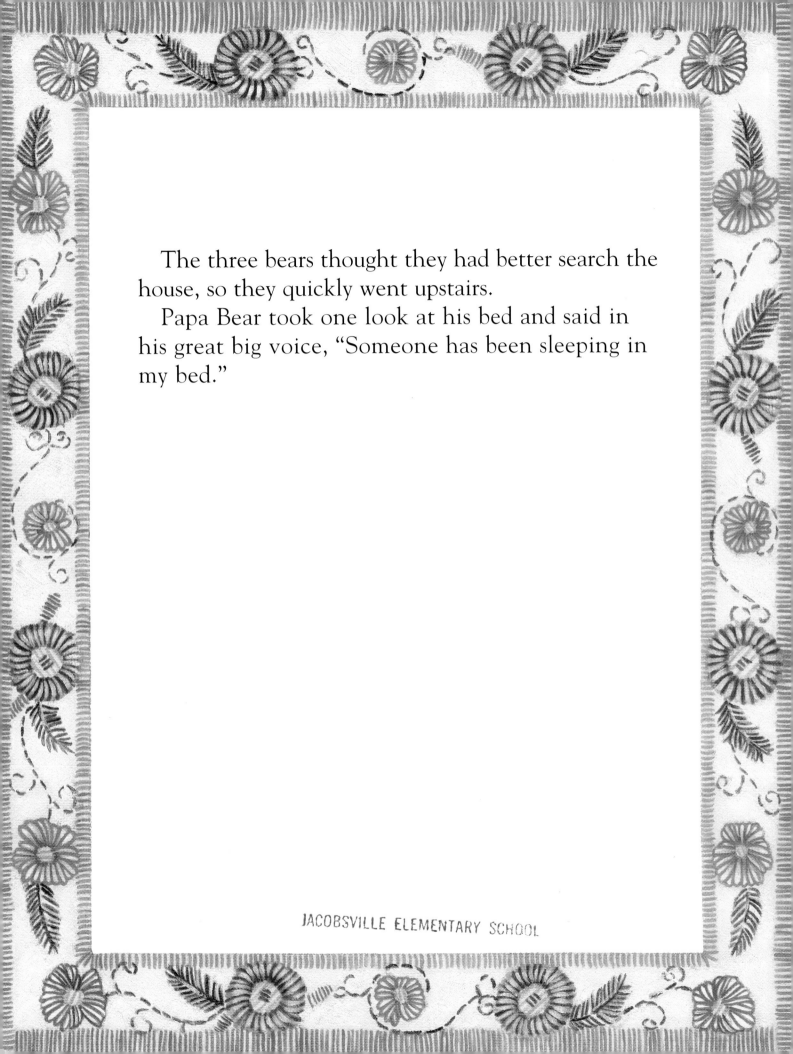

The three bears thought they had better search the house, so they quickly went upstairs.

Papa Bear took one look at his bed and said in his great big voice, "Someone has been sleeping in my bed."

Mama Bear looked at her bed and said in her medium-size voice, "Someone has been sleeping in my bed as well."

Then Baby Bear said as loud as he could, "Someone has been sleeping in my bed, too, and here she is!"

With that Goldilocks awoke with a fright.

This is what she saw.

"Oh my!" shrieked Goldilocks, and she lept from the bed. She ran past the three startled bears, down the stairs, and out the front door.

She ran and ran as fast as her legs would carry her, all through the woods and all the way home.

And the three bears never saw Goldilocks again.

ABOUT THE AUTHOR/ILLUSTRATOR

❖   ❖   ❖

Janice Russell is a portrait painter, decorative
painter, and interior designer. She is the owner
of Russell, a design firm specializing in clocks,
furniture, dinnerware, and tile murals.
Ms. Russell lives in New York City.